Heartburn

Damien Casey

Special thanks to Wendy Dalrymple.

Her cute little romance books made me think, "Hey, I bet those are fun to write!"

They are.

If you hate this, blame Wendy

K Thx

Note:

I'm not trying to make fun of anyone here
but just provide a mutual spot for us all to
laugh at ourselves a little.
The dates included are based on what I
think are the most annoying, loud, and toxic
parts of fandoms. Not the fandoms
themselves as a whole.
You'll find things I absolutely ADORE being
laughed at too.
So please, if you find yourself saying
"Damien is a dickhead! He thinks that
everyone who likes _______ is _______!"
Not true. I believe we're all beautiful people
who deserve to be loved and appreciated for
our differences.
That doesn't mean that I don't think we
should at least be able to laugh at the people
on Twitter who like the same stuff as us but
say the stupidest shit.
These dates are made to represent the most
elitist, gatekeeping, toxic parodies of
fandoms. These people aren't real, these are
just exaggerations of the goofiest of us.
You can always reach out and call me an
asshole though if you want and I will talk to
you, listen, and apologize if I have truly
upset you.
Love and kisses.

Prologue

ana Ripley was bored, tired, lonely, and absolutely sick to death of hearing about her friend, Barb's, sexploitations every night.

Dana wasn't looking for a quick hump and farewell, though. She wanted something that would maybe last. At thirty-three she was tired of one-night stands with whatever guy or girl tickled her fancy. She needed companionship that counted for more than her cat, Sir Kurt Russel the Third, and his judging eyes over not having food in his bowl at 7:30 am.

Listen, why can't cats have opposable thumbs and save us all the time?

"Hey, sis," says Barb from the other room. "Check out this app."

"What app?" Dana asks.

"The one I sent you a link for."

"I haven't got a link."

"Just give it a minute."

She runs her fingers through her curly hair while she waits for the text tone to go off.

A cat meows and she checks her phone.

Ten-in-Ten

Ten blind dates in ten days.

That's the description of the app.

She fills out a quick survey about her personality, what she's looking for, and her interests. The app tells her it will arrange some dates and email her in the morning.

"It's going to get back to me!" She yells.

"Do what now?" says Barb from the other room.

"The app!"

"Oh! Do you need me to send it again?"

"No… I got it!"

"It's pretty easy! I got laid eight nights in a row because of that app!"

No, thinks Dana, *it's probably because you work out at four in the fucking morning everyday, so you look like a girl from a Brazilian Butt Lift commercial or one of those girls who keep popping up in my explore page on Instagram.*

Look at one babe's profile and your whole algorithm is absolutely fucked.

It also probably helps Barb that she's extremely physical, and extremely horny. Like seriously, how far can too far go? When's this girl going to get it out of her system.

Dana sleeps that night thinking about how good it would be if this app helped her meet the man or woman of her dreams in ten days. Can't one of these people just show up in armor riding a horse with a sign that reads "here to save you from a cold lonely and mediocre death?"

She checks her phone as soon as she wakes up.

Her ten dates are set.

Oh joy.

One:
Who's a fucking fish?

The first date has Dana meeting a man named William at a small bar and grill. She walks in and is seated at a booth.

She looks over the menu and orders a stout to keep her company on her wait.

She prefers something a little lighter than the sludge from the inside of a chimney in 1856 but this place only has weird ass IPAs.

That shit tastes like someone mowed their lawn and used carbonated water to catch the clippings. She doesn't want anything to do with that.

A man walks up wearing green slacks, a button-down flannel shirt, and a slight smile.

She finds him attractive enough in a "guy who looks like he may either be a lumberjack or a bowler" kind of way.

"Hey, my names William," he says.

"Dana," she says shaking the hand he extends.

"Did you order a drink? I'll tell you; this place has the best raspberry IPAs. They're made by this really small local brewery."

"Yeah, Four Brothers and A Dad Brewery, right? I've been there a few times."

"It's a really small place, about a half hour from here."

"I've been there."

"They serve food too. I was going to put that as my preferred destination, but I thought this little place felt more down to Earth. Anyway, I'll take you there next date. You'll love it."

She doesn't bother trying to explain to him again that she's been there. Maybe he missed it in the midst of his over excited mansplaining. She's also thinking he may be a little overconfident to mention a second date right after ignoring her.

Man explains favorite band to woman who is in the band.

"So," William says, "what do you do?"

"Hmmm," says Dana, "well, I guess by day I work from home. I do art for magazines and sell some comics to newspapers. I mainly draw. My friend, Barb, she's the writer."

"Ah, a writer! I happen to be a writer myself."

"Really? That's cool. Self-published?"

William spits his IPA into a napkin. He doesn't catch some of it and it speckles Dana's face.

"God, no," he says, "I'm trying to sell my novel to an agent currently. It's a slice of life Americana novel set in 1892 Wyoming. It's about a family who must transport an ill family member to another state so she can be buried."

"*As I Lay Dying*?"

"My mother was a fish."

"Do fucking what now?"

"That's from *As I Lay Dying*."

"Right. Ok. But that's sort of what your book sounds like."

"I like to think of myself as a modern Faulkner. I have researched the depths and intricacies of the average American family in all time periods."

"Interesting."

"I fancy myself more of a… how do I say it? I'm more of a scholar in humanity than an author."

"Very neat."

Dana puts a straw in her stout.

Isn't that supposed to get you drunk, like, hella fast?

She's thinking she'll have to be drunk AF to finish this one.

"Ok, Dana," he says, "now that I know what you do to extend your human condition. What is it you do for you. For your spirit. For your soul. For you, GODDAMNIT!" He slams his hand on the table hard trying to make a point with the profanity. "What is it that you do for Dana?"

"Ok… wow… so… I make book covers for self-published authors, and I make album art for bands sometimes."

"I dare say, the writers are not deserving of your beauty. If your work is half the work of art as your face… their writing would never match. That would be like selling a wine bottle filled with Yoo-hoo, a caviar made from Tootsie Rolls. Put a sign on it that says 'warning, content does not match the expertly crafted art on the front'"

"Uh… weird… but… thanks… Will."

"It's William."

"Ok… sorry."

"I refuse to go by anything other than my proper name. I have an uncle who does me a great disservice by calling me Willy. Can you believe that? A college professor named Willy."

"Wow. What a shame."

"I'm sure after dinner and conversation, you'll be ok with seeing my… Willy."

"Ok. I think I'm done here. Check please."

Dana stands to leave, waving at the waiter. William, definitely not Willy, waves the waiter away.

"A badly timed joke," he says.

Against her better judgement, Dana sits back down and gives him one single foul for his nerves.

"So, where are you from William?"

"Uptown. I have a small one-bedroom apartment."

"I love it uptown! I've seen hella good bands up there."

"Mmmm. I used to enjoy that type of music, but now I find myself listening to a more sentimental music. I prefer the great singer songwriters of our time like Guthrie, Petty, and Waits. That music sounds like a bunch of cavemen smashing their instruments to my ears nowadays."

"I watched Against Me! uptown when they were touring for their last album. It was great."

"I heard the commotion while I was trying to write."

"Right."

"Yep. I was writing."

The waiter comes over to take their order. Dana says she's not quite ready yet. She's assuming this guy is going to piss her off again. He's got a real air about him.

"Dana," he asks, "are you familiar with the film, *In Bruges*?"

"Ok, seriously, check," Dana means it that time. She can take his gross advances, every dude does that. But one thing she absolutely cannot and will not take is being on a date with a dude who wants to explain the symbolism of that movie.

The bars are just bars, it was just a filming angle, it wasn't showing how a character freed himself from his inner prison. Just watch a movie. Not everything has to mean something. Fuck.

She pays for both of their drinks and stands to leave.

William does the same.

"What are you doing?" she asks.

"Isn't this the part where you're so overcome with me that we go back to my apartment, and I ravage you multiple times?"

"No," says the waiter, "it isn't. You ruined the date, dude."

"Yeah? What do you know? You probably haven't even read Faulkner."

"I have. He's shit."

"Who do you like then? Stephen fucking King? Get real, man. Grow up."

"Yeah, I do."

"Oh."

"Yeah."

"I'm sorry."

"That's ok."

"Cool."

"Sorry about your date, for what it's worth."

"Thanks. That means a lot. Do you think I overdid it? Was she maybe intimidated by my intelligence?"

"Nah, I think she thought you were one pretentious mother fucker. She tipped me twenty dollars though. That's why I've kept you distracted enough for her to get away."

William looks around.

Dana is nowhere to be found.

That's because she's already in an Uber laughing her ass off about some dude who thought *In Bruges* was going to be a total panty dropper.

Two:

Fuck Jim Cornette

Last night was awful. Surely tonight wouldn't be THAT bad?

Dana decided to straighten her usually curly hair for this one.

The guy had his recommended spot at a sports bar, so she threw on jeans and a pair of Vans.

The guy's page said he was a wrestling fanatic, and if there's one thing she's learned by living with Barb, it's about wrestling. Barb takes up every inch of the front room on Monday, Tuesday, Wednesday, Friday, and some Saturdays and Sundays watching the stuff.

Dana has become partial to AEW because of the wrestler Willow Nightingale; she's just all smiles and ass kicking.

Barb says she doesn't get the "push" she deserves.

Dana doesn't care.

She just really likes watching it.

With that in mind she throws on a shirt that reads "nothing matters, smile anyway" and heads out the door to impress this date.

Surely wearing a Willow Nightingale shirt will impress a hardcore wrestling fan.

Her date beat her here this time and he's flagging her down from a booth just inside the door.

Well, at least he's excited to see her.

"Wow!" he says "you look way different than your pic. In a good way though."

"Thank you," Dana reaches her hand out to shake.

The guy brushes his hand on the side of his jeans and does the same.

She reads his shirt.

Suplex city.

Great.

"You like Brock?" she asks.

"You like wrestling?"

She holds her shirt out like it's some badge of honor that he should instantly recognize.

She's a little bummed because he is cute. He's tall, has long curly hair, and seems fit.

"I'm not familiar with that name," he says.

"She's on AEW," Dana says.

"Oh… I don't really watch that."

"Why not? I love it."

"I don't like new school flippy stuff. I also don't like modern women's wrestling a lot."

"Ok. I need an explanation there because Britt has been killing it."

"She's only there because of her boyfriend."

"Who is that?"

"Adam Cole."

"You do realize you're talking to a woman right now and you've already given me like three red flags before I've even ordered chicken wings, right?"

"So, you know then. Women shouldn't be bleeding on tv in matches. It's unattractive."

"I didn't know women were only supposed to be wrestling to be attractive."

They sit there in awkwardness for a bit longer.

Goddamn t-shirt was a horrible idea.

Made this guy show his douche bag in five seconds flat.

"This was bad," Dana says, "let's start over. I'm Dana."

"I'm Ray."

"Nice to meet you."

"I looked her up."

"Who?"

"Willow Nightingale."

"Cool! She's awesome!"

"I don't know. I don't like people like her and Jordynne Grace. One is out of shape and the other looks like a man."

"Ok. What the fuck is your problem? I tried to save you and you're STILL shooting yourself in the foot. Ask me about literally anything else. What about your parents?"

"I love my parents. I'm staying with them right now. I'm kind of between jobs."

"Such is the economy. My parents run a newspaper in a small town up north. It's fun to go back and visit their office. They just listen to podcasts all day and edit a newspaper. Do you like podcasts?"

"I like the Jim Cornette podcast."

"What's that?"

"A wrestling podcast."

"My friend Barb is a bigger fan than me. Let me ask her if she's familiar with it."

Barb texts back "RUN" when Dana asks.

Dana stands up and just flat-out leaves.

It works out perfectly because she hasn't even ordered a drink yet.

If Barb is saying run, she better just run.

"Hey!" says Ray behind her. "I didn't mean to offend you. I think women have just as much a spot in wrestling as men. I have like, an Alexa Bliss shirt at home even."

"Yeah? She's actually pretty good."

"See. Plus, she looks great. That's all I mean. I want it to be believable. Like the men should be fit and so should the women. That's all."

Dana stands outside of a sports bar wishing she had said she was using the restroom. This guy isn't making much sense. He may as well say "women should be seen… and only then when they're attractive" because he's just really blowing it.

"I just like the older wrestling," he says. "You know, where it was believable. I don't like all of this modern comedy stuff. I want wrestling to be believable."

"Do you like the Undertaker?"

"Yeah," Ray opens the door thinking he's won her back. "He's one of the best of all time."

"He could teleport, Ray."

He stares at her confused.

Apparently, believability takes a beach vacation for the goddamn Undertaker.

"People can't really teleport. It's a shame this didn't work out. I had this whole thing planned where I was going to call you my ray of sunshine."

"You're a bitch."

"I assumed you'd say something like that. K byyyyeeee."

Dana gets in her car and slams her forehead against the steering wheel. The Brock Lesnar shirt should have been the red flag.

Should have been the big old Brock Lobster so to speak.

When she gets home, Barb checks her over to make sure she isn't corrupted.

"Britt Baker?"

"Yes."

"The Young Bucks?"

"Amazing."

"Kennnnyyyy Ommmmmeeeggggaaaaaa!"

"Best bout machine."

"Ok ok you seem ok. Now tell me. Who is better? Mandy Rose… or Bayley?"

"Bayley."

"Oh, thank god."

Barb annoyingly fake faints on the couch.

"People who listen to Cornette are the Trumpers of the wrestling world. I thought for sure everything I taught you was going to be ruined. What did he look like?"

"Tall, curly hair, fit, he was cute. His name was Ray."

"RAY?!" Barb makes a fake gagging sound. "He was literally in my DMs yesterday asking if we could go out. How fucking gross! He likes the NWA! THE MODERN NWA!"

Dana shrugs and heads to her room to doodle a little before she passes out.

She ends up drawing a giant sweaty man with a T-bone steak for a head.

Three:
That one level in Battletoads is really hard.

Barb gave her pepper spray tonight.

After hearing they let people who like Jim Cornette on the app, she wasn't about to let Dana leave the house without some sort of protection.

She should have some anyway, Barb told her all about how annoying her lack of safety was for ten minutes straight.

Seriously, it was like an alarm went off at exactly ten minutes.

The date tonight was with a guy named Kerry. His bio said his main interest was video games. Barb was worried that meant he sat around playing *Call of Duty* in his mom's basement while chugging Monster energy drinks all day.

Dana knew that wasn't the case, thankfully, when she pulled up to an arcade.

It was one of those hella cool places that lets you play *DigDug* while drinking and Dana was STOKED. She made Barb play *Mortal Kombat 2* at one last year for around three hours straight.

Dana- 103

Barb- 0

The squat down then uppercut method has never once failed her.

She finds Kerry playing *BattleToads* and drinking some blue mixture. She walks over, says hi, tells him she's getting a drink.

Maybe he's deaf in his right ear because he didn't respond.

He's shorter than her, quite a bit wider, and he has long straight blonde hair. He's clean though, and he smells alright. The rest is irrelevant to her. She wouldn't be out here on this ridiculous ten in ten mission if she based everything on looks.

When she comes back with a local stout, she sets it on the table beside the game and asks if he wants to play two player. He sighs and presses start for her.

They play for around fifteen minutes.

Neither saying a word.

"This is great," Dana says. "I always wanted a date that didn't talk."

"Sorry," Kerry says as he ends the game. "I get really into gaming."

"I can see that. I love *Mortal Kombat 2*. My little brother used to always want to spend time with me and my friends. I would say 'if you can beat me, you can hang out all night.' Then I'd use the squat down, wait 'til he gets close, then uppercut method. He never beat me once. He even tried using Baraka."

"I don't really want to date anyone."

"Oh?"

"My mom said I needed to get out of the house for something other than work, so I signed up for the app. I'm actually a furry and only date other furries."

"So, like, an animal dressing person?"

"Yes."

"How do you… you know?"

"I'm prepared."

With that he fires up *Killer Instinct* and says, "that way of playing *Mortal Kombat* is cheating, by the way."

Dana drinks three more beers and starts feeling buzzed enough to act like a fool.

She pulls down her V-neck so that her cleavage is out and on display. The top half of her boobs are the glue in the cheese of a pizza commercial. She's never seen anyone watch one of those and not have a craving for a slice.

She asks him to play *Carn-Evil* with her. He looks right at her tits and mumbles "sure."

They play in silence for another fifteen minutes. She has to admit, he's pretty damn good at games.

"Well, I think I'm going to go now. I have a raid with some friends in a couple hours. One of them is going to a con so I want to make sure I get to know her better. You understand?"

"Sure. But I'm right here. I'm in person. I'll give you another chance because I'm desperate. Straight up. If you can beat me at *Mortal Kombat 2*… I'll buy you dinner, take you back to my place, where we can play *Super Mario 3*, or something on the Switch… then I will probably sleep with you because… why not?"

She doesn't mean this.

Well, she means most of it except the sleeping with part.

That part has potential if he can actually start forming sentences. Maybe he's just nervous AF?

He agrees to this.

After taking another eye full of cleavage.

He loses five times.

Thanks, uppercut method.

He gets mad and says she cheated so therefore she should sleep with him.

Dana closes her eyes, sighs, then just leaves.

"I told you," says Barb at home, "dudes on that app are only trying to get laid, or please their parents or something. You'll never stand a chance."

"I don't get it," Dana says. "I have a date with ANOTHER guy tomorrow. Fourth night in a row. I put that I'm Bi so why isn't it matching me with other women?"

"Because women are too smart to use that app, Dana."

"Hi. Nice to meet you. I'm a woman."

"Not a smart one."

Dana goes to her room and screams into a pile of pillows.

Four:

Totino's pizza rolls

The wood on this bench is all worn down.

Dana is already dreading asking Barb to pull splinters out of her ass.

Why do these idiots use this bench when they have three other benches in the skatepark?

She knew this was a bust before she ever showed up. Dude had skateboarding under his hobbies and his preferred meet up was a public park for a picnic... sounds great until you realize there's also a skatepark there... and you have to put a meal of some sort as your preferred date. What meal did he put?

His name is Graham and he told her he had to finish up his "exercising routine" and then they would have a picnic.

He even had a towel and a Walmart bag with food in it.

There's the meal.

It's April.

That food isn't going to last in the weird Ohio heatwave that happens mid-April.

His friends are trying so hard to give him advice…

"Dude, that babe is waiting on you."

"She wore a tank top just so you'd notice her tits and you're over here with us."

"Are you a homo?"

That one annoyed her. Maybe he is gay? Maybe he's afraid to come out because the weird toxic masculinity of high school sports has somehow trickled its way into skateboarding.

She thinks if it's at the Olympics it was only a matter of time before the toxic masculinity invaded and tried to take over. Here it is on full display. This isn't the same skateboarding her brother liked; this park seems more like a competition than an art form. She feels more like she's watching football practice after school.

Is this what dating after thirty is like?

Being really judgmental of an entire interest because one person said something shitty?

Or is she just getting bitter?

Graham skates over and hands her the Walmart bag saying, "you can start eating without me. That's fine," and skates away.

Definitely not interested in the date, Dana thinks.

Hopefully he finds what makes him happy at some point, but this plastic bag with a box of pizza rolls that have lightly thawed in the sun isn't it.

She takes one of the bottles of Mountain Dew and starts doing a lap around the park back to her car.

She hears the other skaters making fun of their friend.

She feels bad about that, but at the same time justified. He wasted her time, toxic masculinity or no toxic masculinity, he still made her waste an hour of her life just so he could keep up some charade that may or may not even be a real thing.

Boredom, she thinks, *leads me to creating all of these scenarios that aren't even real.*

Realistically, he probably thought his kickflip backside 50-50 was going to be IT and he could end his skate session with a babe driving him home and letting him get to third base.

Why don't I just do that? She thinks. *I don't have anything else going on today.*

She thinks about how she's on a date because of her own form of toxic thinking.

Is she fine being single? Sorta.

Is she a little lonely? Sorta.

Is it worth these past four days? Hell no.

She thinks about what her life would be if she just stayed single. She could constantly work on her art. She could hang out with Barb everyday. She could have as many Hermit Crabs as she wants, and no one would say a thing. Kurt the Third would love it.

That's the part that bothers her, though.

Working on art with no one other than Barb to show. How long would that last? Barb will eventually get married and have kids; that's just the type of life she wants to have. Which is fine but doesn't leave a lot of time to make fun of Dana for having a million Hermit Crabs.

Until a week ago she was fine being thirty-three and single. Up until her little brother, little Manny at the age of twenty-nine, announced his engagement. Then life started to catch up and make her feel like she should be doing these things too, right?

She finds herself on the other side of the park from the bench. She hears the skaters calling Graham gay.

"So what if he is?" she speaks up.

"Nothing at all, that's cool, we don't care!" says the skater in an instant change of heart.

"I'm not gay," Graham says, "I just don't want to date a poser."

"Huh?"

"You're wearing Vans… you don't even skate."

"Alllllright. I'm good. See you guys later."

She hurries back to her car. On her way she hears one of them say, "poser or not, did you see the size of her jugs?"

"You date a poser then! What's more important to you, skating or big tits?" Graham replies.

She turns on her car and pulls out of there like she's the last survivor in a slasher film who just so happened to be lucky enough to find a working car.

Barb tells her that her boobs aren't THAT big, it was probably the tank top and lack of seeing other boobs that made those dudes all wild.

Thanks, Barb.

Five:
Tim the Toolman Taylor is an asshole now.

Oddly enough, Dana's fifth date was scheduled in her preferred meetup. Apparently, the app says if you have gone on more dates than the other your place is the place.

Good.

She needed home field advantage.

She chose her favorite burger place because she had a theory; if the person isn't into cheeseburgers, there's no need for a second date.

She picks a booth and slides in, the grease from the deep friers making the covering of the seat feel like a slide covered in oil.

She pretends to look at a menu until she hears a voice say, "Dana?"

Allie is a pleasant surprise from the past four. Right out of the gate she seems… not annoying at all; which is the biggest thing Dana could possibly hope for after the past few nights.

"Allie!" Dana says a little too excitedly. She's already starting to crush a little on the other woman. Slightly shorter than her with straight blonde hair, a leather jacket with horror movie pins, a *Killer Klowns from Outer Space* shirt, and a pair of black jeans.

She's like an Angel sent from bad date heaven to rescue her on the fifth date.

"I've never been here before," Allie says. "Has to be better than last night. This guy took me to this arcade… nevermind. Let's not start this thing off with gossip."

"Please do. Was his name Kerry, by chance?"

"YES! He wouldn't even play the *Jurassic Park* game with me!"

"I got him to play *Carn-Evil*, but then he was pissed because I beat him in *Mortal Kombat 2*."

"YOU'RE THE UPPERCUT CHICK?!?!"

"What can I say? A good strategy never fails."

"Holy shit. I told him I wanted to marry you when I was leaving just to piss him off."

"If it's a proposal, the answer is yes."

"Deal."

They both laugh.

Dana secretly thinks she wouldn't say no if it was a proposal. But as is life on this Ten-in-Ten app, something has to be a miss. What's wrong with Allie? Is she a collector of coins that passed through the state of Wyoming and she will spend the whole evening talking about how she knows they came through Wyoming? Is she obsessed with some obscure nineties TV show that no one can stand? Or worse, does she eat Pickles?

"I'll have the double western with NO pickles," Allie orders alleviating that fear.

"I hate pickles," Dana says, reaching for any conversational piece she can find.

"They're GNARLY. It's like eating a sour candy pretending to be a vegetable."

The way she says vegetables is even attractive to Dana.

Vej-uh-tuh-bulls.

"I like your shirt," Dana says. "My roommate, Barb, and me, we always have bad horror movie fridays."

"Oh, what are you planning for tomorrow?"

"I don't know. It's her pick. Last week I picked *Demon Wind*."

"The one that had the holographic cover and the magician?"

"The EXACT one."

"I haven't seen it in YEARS!"

The conversation flows through bad horror movies, to bad dates from the app again, to milkshakes, to talking about each other's personal life.

"I was raised by a single dad," says Allie, "he did his best, but he was twenty when I was born so I've had a LOT of practice with the bad date carousel from just watching him."

"My parents are still happily married. Cringingly happy. My brother and I always pick on them and say they're actually robots."

"Do robots even mate?"

"That's a good question. I feel like, no? Wouldn't they just build their kids?"

"I think so. Unless they took some of their own parts. You have your father's eyes, literally. He's blind now. He took them out and gave them to you."

"Damn, I better get him a good gift for Father's Day."

The robot talk leads into day job talk. Allie works at a radio station; not as the DJ but in communications.

She thinks Dana's art is hella cool, she even has to admit she picked up a piece at a convention one time and didn't recognize her.

The piece was a recreated movie poster for the movie *Galaxy Quest*.

They chat about everything for another hour until they're given complementary coffee. The age old "hey, you should maybe think about leaving now" from the staff.

They sip the coffee and continue chatting. Allie tells the waiter they don't need anything, pays the bill, leaves a nice tip, and then explains to the staff they can clean up around them, they really don't mind.

The staff does just that and before long they're surrounded by tables with chairs put up and can't leave until the freshly mopped floor dries.

They leave with the staff and make their way next door to a quiet pub.

Both order stouts and choose a small booth to continue talking in.

They both cringe when they see a poor girl on a date with another guy they both know, William.

He waved at them nervously and continues chatting the girl's ear off about whatever boring bullshit he's draining her in.

Dana stands up on tired, wobbly, buzzed legs and heads over to the table.

She's going to be a lifeguard tonight, no one is drowning under a sea of pretentiousness on her watch.

"William!" she says, "this is my cousin! She's great. Come sit with us for a bit! William won't care if you come visit, will you?"

"Actually," William says, "we're kind of talking about the seminal works of American fiction-"

"Sorry, William," says the woman, "I haven't seen her in forever! I'm going to go visit for a few, I'll be right back!"

When Dana and the woman get back to the table all three just start hysterically laughing about William Faulkner and how shitty boring his work was.

After they laugh for a solid five minutes, William's date sees him go to the bar.

She makes a shrug motion and runs out the front door.

The prison guard dropped the ball for two seconds and the prisoner escaped.

Fearing the awkwardness of that conversation, and seeing its 1:27am, Dana and Allie decide to flee as well.

When they're outside Allie trips over her own untied shoelace.

"Ah, no," she says bending over. "I never learned how to do this. I just always wear slip-ons or Velcro. My roommate said I had to look nice and having laces in your shoes is nice."

"It is sort of a very basic test. Can this person tie their shoes."

"This person cannot."

"That's ok, hold on."

Dana stumbles around, finally feeling the alcohol catching up to her and takes every bit of five minutes to tie the shoe. All filled with "wait, shit, hold on, I think, no, goddamnit."

When she stands up, she takes a deep breath and announces she better get an Uber tonight.

Allie shows her her phone screen, two cars are on their way for each of them.

"You'll have to tell yours where to go, I didn't know that."

Dana leans in and kisses Allie.

This was the best night she's had in a long time, she wanted to end it with confirmation.

Allie smiles and says, "yeah, I've had a great night too."

"Should we keep doing these awful dates or just call it now?"

"Let's keep doing them, and then every night we can vent to each other. That should bring us closer, like when two people go through something traumatic together."

"I like that. How many do you have left?"

"Six. None of them are going to matter now."

"I have five and I feel the same way. Can I call you Al?"

"Like from *Home Improvement*?"

"Exactly like from *Home Improvement*. My little handyman fixing up all the mistakes that other guy makes."

"I need to buy more flannel."

The first Uber arrives, Allie helps Dana into it. They exchange phone numbers and wave goodbye.

Dana sleeps soundly that night.

Six:
Make America intolerant of bigots again.

"So, yeah, that's why I think abortion should be banned," says the guy in flannel, Dave?

Dana can't remember. As soon as he turned up in a hat about the 2nd amendment, she tuned him out.

For the better that this guy showed up blowing his chance for a second date instantly anyway; her mind was still on last night.

She was riding the waves of puppy love all the way through the next five dates. That's what she planned.

This one for sure.

This guy had some weirdo alpha male bullshit going on about him.

He talked about how Critical Race Theory was bad for a little while, transitioned into how white males are being oppressed now, then he went into guns, he just ended his rant about abortion.

Dana only heard a little of it.

She knew if she even tried to disagree or debate with this guy he'd call her some insult that had to do with being a liberal.

There's a difference between being liberal and being just a decent human being who believes people should be able to do whatever they want as long as it isn't ruining another person's right to live the way they want to.

Long and short… she doesn't care what her neighbor is doing as long as it isn't hurting the neighborhood.

This guy, this… Dave… all he wants to do is deport the neighborhood it seems like.

Doesn't matter.

In about five minutes she's going to stand up and leave. She wanted to when he mentioned critical race theory; but being a woman would have only made that worse.

Then he'd be playing the victim card to his buddies later as they all sat around huffing gasoline, listening to Joe Rogan, and worshipping the confederate flag.

Fucking idiots.

She decided she'd let the guy pay for the cheese sticks she ate.

She had to listen to his tirade about same sex marriage, didn't she?

Even when she said she was Bisexual all she got was "you're leaving already?" Dude didn't want a date; he wanted a platform to spew bullshit and Dana happened to be the unlucky one to show up for improv night at the dipshit comedy club.

The worst part is this guy is for real.

He really thinks the shit he's saying.

He really thinks he's the manliest man of America.

He really thinks people like him are the future of the world.

Good luck with that, most people are getting smart enough to stop reproducing with dipshits like this.

Marjorie Taylor Greene can only take on so many spouses before Lauren Boebart is going to have to start picking up the slack.

The bigot simp club.

"Did you see where Boebart said xenophobic shit about Ilhan Omar?"

"Yeah boy! Totally gave me a boner!"

Fucking losers.

She spends the back half of the date texting back and forth with Allie.

"Do you need your shoes tied before your big date?" She sends.

"Only if you have time to stop by and tie them," replies Allie. "The guy I'm meeting tonight is into fixing computers."

"Nice. He probably has all the best porn then."

"His username is 'Keyboard Cowboy.'"

"Yikes."

"I'll keep you posted on the cowboy part."

She laughs loud enough for Dave to notice she isn't paying attention.

"Sorry," he says. "Tell me about your life, what do you believe in?"

"Bigfoot."

"What?"

"I believe in Bigfoot."

"Oh…"

"And aliens."

"I believe in reptilians. There's a whole slew of them-"

"And the Loch Ness Monster."

"Do you believe in America?"

"That has got to be the corniest shit anyone has ever said to me."

Dave just stares at her.

She checks her face to see if any marinara sauce is there and realizes she doesn't care.

"What DO you like about America?" she asks.

"I love America."

"Seems fishy to me. You hate poor people, you think women are inferior, you don't believe anyone who isn't a straight white male deserves any freedom, you hate people who came here from other places, you don't like the way people want to change the medical system, you don't like around 78% of the population… so what do you love so much other than guns, bigotry, and being a simp for the rich?"

"You're a liberal, aren't you?"

"Ugh. Lauren Boebart is a bitch."

"You ARE a liberal!"

"Marjory Taylor Green is about half stupid too, and that's the good half!"

Dave continues to stare in absolute shock.

"Now," Dana says. "I'm leaving. And you're going to pay for my cheese sticks and soda because that's the very LEAST you can do for ruining my entire night."

"A freeloading liberal. I should have guessed that's why you're single."

"And you're probably single because every woman in your life is laughing at you. Laughing at how you think people like you, who can't even figure out that scientists are smarter than them, are going to restore

America to some past glory. The civil war ended, and you all lost, go get fucked."

She turns and walks away from the table before turning back to say, "also, your flannel doesn't match your hat. Usually, that's no big deal, but in this case, they clash and make you look like you don't own a mirror. K byyyyeeee."

She checks her phone when she gets to her car.

One message from Allie.

"He's legitimately wearing a cowboy hat and chaps."

Seven:
The theater seating is at least comfy.

The thing about a blind date is usually you don't even know who you're meeting until you show up. The Ten-in-Ten app shows a name, some background info, and a meeting spot. The app keeps photos and other personal info of course, just in case, you know.

Dana thought a blind date would mean that you could at least see and speak to your date. Five out of six could have been better the way this one is; dark, dinner with a movie playing, and no one talking about any bullshit.

She met Dylan inside the theater. She was running a little behind because she was talking to Allie on the phone about their future dates.

Allie was meeting a football fan at Buffalo Wild Wings.

Dana was meeting this self-proclaimed movie nut.

He was in his seat, already eating a personal pizza. He had dark blonde hair, a full beard, and a gazey look in his eyes.

She apologized for being late, and he accepted it. He told her they were watching one of his favorite David Lynch movies, and before she could finish her dinner order the lights went down.

She sat there, watching this movie she'd seen before, trying to figure out what it was about. She kept just getting annoyed about how so many people think it's one of the best things ever put to fucking film.

Stupid ass chicken dance scene.

Fucking tiny hens.

She pushed through hoping that maybe she could chat with the guy after the date, but he kept checking his phone during the movie and laughing at texts from someone named "Samantha."

Now that the movie is over, they sit in the theater's bar and sip on their respective beers and stare at their phones. Dylan laughs in between asking if Dana likes this movie or that movie.

Dana checks her phone for messages from Allie between saying yes or no.

Each time she says yes, Dylan goes off on a tangent about the directors' other films. He started linking everything back to the movies he liked, and she just got so annoyed. She didn't care how many degrees of actor/director/producer/sequel Tremors was from fucking Inland Empire.

Tremors is pretty damn cool.

Inland Empire was ranked slightly above the Transformers franchise for her; pretty damn low.

She just wasn't a David Lynch fan.

She knows you either love the guy's stuff or hate it, she falls mostly into the hate it section and she gets the vibe Dylan is picking up on it.

"Do you like Don Dohler?" she asks.

"Who?" he asks.

"The director."

"Never heard of him."

"*The Alien Factor?*"

"Nope."

"*Fiend?*"

"Huh uh."

"*Fiend* is the longest movie ever made but it's only an hour and twenty minutes.

"I don't get it."

"You would if you had ever seen *Fiend*."

"What kind of films?"

"Oh, these are MOVIES, not films. You get what I mean?"

"No."

"These movies lack any sense of pretentiousness. They're made by a guy with a home video camera and the most bitchin' practical effects you'll ever see for a monster."

"So, like John Carpenter's *The Thing*?"

See, Dana thinks, *who the fuck says that and not just The Thing? Dude is cringe.*

"Nowhere near it. We're talking a budget of $1000 that was spent of a monster suit."

"…oh."

"Best movies you'll ever see."

"Do you like Tarantino? He makes stuff like that. I love Tarantino."

Dana spits her beer in laughter.

"No, no. Tarantino does NOT make movies like that. Tarantino makes pretentious movies parading as Grindhouse features where he writes his own dialogue so he can say the n-word and get away with it."

"I think given the nature of the movies-"

"The man is AWFUL. He has his head so far up his own ass."

They both crack a disappointed smile.

This is going to go nowhere good.

Dana stands up and extends her hand, "well, it was nice to meet you, Dylan. I hope your next date works out better."

"Nice to meet you, Dana. I actually had a really great night with someone last night. So, I apologize if I've been really distant."

"It's ok, I had one of those a few nights ago."

They awkwardly shake and part ways. Dana has a text from Allie.

"My date was awful. The guy thought I should know what a Joe Burrow is. I do, but I pretended to not to get under his skin."

Dana takes a gamble and sends back, "my place at ten?"

Interlude for an awkward sex scene.

They watched *The Alien Factor* together.

Eventually their lips found each other, their hands found each other, their beings linked together in the glow of the TV screen in the shadow of the Lemoid.

It was awkward at first, they stumbled over one another, they clanked their teeth together a couple times.

Dana couldn't figure out Allie's bra.

Allie couldn't figure out how to unbutton Dana's top.

Eventually they both found the roadmap of each other's bodies and enjoyed the night.

The Alien Factor was left on repeat until they woke up the next morning laughing hysterically.

Eight:
So forlorn.

She has been talking for a solid ten minutes but Dana can't hear her over the overly loud bass in her ears.

Who knew a Bauhaus song could sound like a rave.

Anything probably could if you turned it up that loud and maxed the bass out. It all just sounded like rumbling with Peter Murphy popping in to say something cryptic here and there.

Hello.

Nice to meet you.

Eat jelly sandwiches and barbed wire.

Cool.

Will do.

She starts laughing about this morning when Allie met Sir Kurt Russel the Third. She asked where the other two were, just like everyone does.

She loves when she tells them he is the first in his lineage and much like the *Street Fighter* franchise, it was better to start on a sequel.

Kurt the Third did his classic jump on a stranger's lap when they're just trying to relax and scared the shit out of Allie.

He's the size of four regular cats, black and white fur, with a chunk of white covering half of his nose making his face seem lopsided.

Allie jumped and spilled her coffee on him, which at this point was lukewarm. Kurt the Third just looked up at her in that judgmental way that only cats can do. His eyes said, "why have you ruined my perfectly clean coat of fur with this… bean water?"

Judgmental little fucker could have at least waited until the coffee was on the table again.

"Is my suffering funny to you as well?" asks the woman sitting across from her. She's eating vegan chili dogs in a goth club;

she's on the next level of suffering and it really IS kind of funny to Dana.

Of course, everything is kind of funny to Dana right now, even the cat story that wouldn't usually be funny. She's on cloud seven hundred and thirty-six right now.

"No," Dana says, "I don't think so. I just thought about my cat."

"I used to have a cat."

"Oh, what happened?"

"It ran away. Even a cat can't stand to be around me. I don't know why I'm even trying on this app. You've probably already met someone better than me."

"Yep! Her name is Allie! Let me tell you, we've been having so much fun together. She met my cat this morning."

"I'll die cold and alone on this bleak Earth."

"Jeez, just mix in a little Meghan Trainor with your Christian Death and you'll be ok!"

"I despise being alive."

"Listen, are you ok?"

"Better than you."

"No, I don't think so."

"I'm not the one dating a juggalo."

"Excuse me?"

"I went on a date a few months ago with Allie. Met her on this app. In this club. She's a juggalo."

"Ok… that's a sort of weirdo accusation to throw at me to make me feel bad. Anyway, what do you do for fun? Let's talk."

"Watch YouTube videos of babies crying. When they realize the life of a human is more painful than that of a flea drowning in a pound of shit, they break down under the weight of the world."

"Wow. You're really intense, you know that?"

"I'm sorry."

"No, no. I like it. Tell me some more sad shit."

She texts Allie almost every single thing this girl is saying. She's talking about some bleak empty eternal suffering level shit and

Dana is looking at the picture she took of Kurt the Third with Allie.

She looks up from her phone and sees the woman whose name she's already forgotten staring at her.

"You're a horrible date, you know that?" the woman says. Her whole demeanor has changed. Even her voice has gone from slow and deep like Dracula into upbeat and high pitched like your stereotypical valley girl. "I can't believe I told you about the things I told you about."

"Oh, erm, I'm sorry."

"I told you about nothing. You've been distracted and boring. I brought you to the best club."

Dana looks around and sees people dancing with glow sticks.

Glow sticks in a goth club.

It's a new one for her.

"And you, you can't even buy me a drink?"

"I thought it would make you sad."

"You think this is a fucking costume? It's a way of life!"

"I'm sorry, are you for real real depressed because, like, I'm totally into going somewhere and talking. If you need to vent or get some advice… I got you."

"No, I'm ok."

"I mean, you were talking about crying babies."

"I'm a goth. That's what we do."

"Are you sure? I went to school with a goth guy, and he just really liked Anne Rice and Sisters of Mercy."

"My wardrobe reflects how I feel on the inside. A withered plant. A curled up and dead calf rotting under the winter sun. It's skin frozen but somehow burnt."

"Yeah. Totally."

"Hey, Jenna!" says a guy coming over and standing by their table. "I thought you had some date tonight!"

"Ahem." says Dana.

"Oh shit! Far out! Totally a babe! And a normie! Why do normies always want a big tit goth girlfriend?"

"Roland!" says Jenna a little too loud and full of life. "Fuck off."

"Oh, right. Sorry!" He turns his attention to Dana and says, "I'm kinda new to this whole thing, I'm not like depressed or anything, well, no more than everyone is, I think. I had a few heavy bouts a year or so ago, but I've really found my people here and couldn't be happier!"

Dana smiles at Jenna who is downright scowling.

"Maybe," says Dana, "Roland should take my seat. I think you could learn a few things from each other."

Dana stands and high fives Roland, yelling in his ear, "you go get your big tit goth girlfriend!"

Roland yells, "YEAH!" and throws Dana another high-five.

Jenna gives her a bird.

The finger kind, not some dead or dying kind.

As Dana leaves the club, she looks back and sees Jenna crack a smile and laugh a little at something Roland said.

"Great," she says to herself, "now I'm Cupid."

"Wanna help me get a date then?" asks the man standing at the door.

Dana just shrugs and walks away.

Nine:
The lord will provide you with a dating app.

Dana was here to meet a guy named Todd.

Todd proudly listed that he was a devout Christian on his page.

That's cool, Dana thinks, as long as he isn't too weird this should be ok.

She realized he was a bit weird when she sat at the table in Olive Garden and had one of those little Christian track books sitting in front of her.

She flipped through the pages wondering why the Hell this guy scheduled a date and then bounced after leaving this?

Did he at least leave money for ravioli?

She looked around for a waiter to ask when she saw a tall guy with brown hair walking toward her. His shirt sported the logo of a local church.

Here he is, she thought, *just like Jesus rising up out of the tomb on Easter Sunday.*

Was Easter when he came back? Or was that when he was crucified? She thought about this all while shaking his hand.

"Dana," he says, "I have to say it's a pleasure to meet you."

"Yeah, this is nice. I really like ravioli."

"Personally, I prefer the meatballs."

She grins and nods.

They sit there awkwardly until the waiter comes and takes their orders.

Neither saying a word.

They just look at each other and do that awkward smile and nod thing like their bodies are saying, "welp, this is awkward."

"I'm sure you noticed," says Todd. "The little pamphlet, comic, type book."

"I did."

"Did you read it?"

"I skimmed."

"We're trying to make those little things

not as old school as they used to be. My church is updating them for younger generations. The old ones were filled with racism, xenophobia, and quite a lot of homophobia."

"You're a pastor?"

"No, I'm just a member of SoulBent church. We used to be called Soul Harvest, but people said it sounded a little creepy."

"That's probably because it does. It sounds like *Children of the Corn* to me."

"Right. Well, we're a pretty open place. We don't care how you dress or if you drink or anything. Our pastor has been known to have a couple Coronas while watching UFC."

"Is that where you work?"

"No. I just want to spread the message of Jesus."

"On a first date."

"I signed up for the app so I could meet people. I was really taken back by the lack of profiles that mentioned anything about purpose or living for God."

"Right. Because it's a dating app. Not really where people are going to post about religion."

"It's a big part of a relationship."

"This is just really awkward, my guy. Did you sign up for this app to meet someone, or did you sign up to use dates as recruitment tools?"

"I signed up just to see how many women would meet me. Then I was like, hey, this could actually help me spread the word of SoulBent."

Dana starts to lay her head on the table just as the waiter shows up with their food.

"Please place the ravioli on my head," she says. The waiter sits it beside her.

Her face is perfectly level with the plate.

She makes eye contact with the ravioli and wonders how in the fuck she got here.

"God loves you," Todd says with a distinct inability to read the room.

Dana lifts her head up and says "how are we paying for dinner? Separate? Am I buying? Are you?"

"I'll get it."

"Ok, let's do this."

She eats the ravioli while he talks about how progressive his church is. How the pastor is young and has tattoos. How they have a rock band that plays every Sunday. He talks about the church events, the trips, the get togethers, the man games.

"Excuse me," Dana says. "Back it up, rewind the tape, what the Hell are the 'Man Games?'"

"That's where men get together and do men stuff. Like smoking meats, throwing axes, eating bacon, you know, man stuff."

"OOF."

"What?"

"Why did bacon go through that weird phase where it was trendy? Remember? There were bacon candles, bacon pillows, bacon lotion, shirts with cringe quotes about bacon, my friend Barb had a bacon bikini. Bacon was like a nationwide meme. Now America is just a giant meme, isn't it?"

"When we have the Man Games the

women usually bring us dinner."

"What about the smoked meats?"

"Sure, but who's going to make the macaroni?"

"Kraft?"

"Not as good."

Dana chows through two plates of endless ravioli. She can feel Todd judging her. She orders a third to go. What's the point of endless if you don't get some for lunch tomorrow?

"It's been nice meeting you, Todd," she says as she stands and lays a fifty on the table. "Take that for mine and leave the leftovers for a tip."

"I was going to leave some comics."

"Something tells me they prefer cash."

She stands and her hip bumps the table sending her half glass of Pepsi spilling into a cardboard box filled with the comics beside the table.

How the fuck did I not notice that, she thinks.

Todd jumps up and grabs the sides of his

head.

All of his work for nothing.

"Oh, shit!" Dana says. "I'm sorry!"

"Maybe if you didn't eat three plates of ravioli this wouldn't have happened."

"That's just downright mean. Maybe if you didn't use a blind dating app as a recruitment app it wouldn't happen, you weird little fucker."

Todd stands up and aggressively takes the box to a big trash can, he slams the box into it and yells "beautiful Jesus grant me the patience!"

Dana quietly whistles through her lips and hurries out of there before the Holy Spirit goes nuclear.

Ten:
Last date, open this pit up.

Denny's is a weird place to see a band.

Her date said it was a punk band, so she was cool with it. Apparently, the manager is in one of the bands, so they let them have shows here sometimes.

She asked Dominik if it was really a punk show after she sat at the table and saw all the camo, black metal shirts, and Nike sneakers.

He said hell yeah, but she didn't believe it.

Now as the first band sets up, she realizes this may be more of a metal or hardcore show.

The band setting up now all have Terror shirts on.

Five Terror shirts, one band.

The people about to watch are doing that thing they do where they stand in a circle because there's about to be moshing in front of the band.

Dominik didn't order food, but she wasn't going to pass up the chance for Eggs Over My Hammy, so she sits here waiting on her food while Dominik punches his fist into his open palm and grills her on bands she likes.

She doesn't like any of them.

"Would you be, like, super offended if I leave after I eat?" she asks. "I just don't really think this is my scene."

"Yo, you better support the bands. Some of them drove from forever away."

"Ok, so yeah, you'll be offended. I'll do my best."

She feels like she's taking her little brother somewhere instead of being on a date.

"You shouldn't eat meat while they're playing," he says. "They're a vegan straight edge band."

"Listen, this feels like the last date I went on. Did you use this app to get more people to come to your shows?"

"Nah, I'm lonely as fuck. I need a date. I just don't know how-"

Before he can finish the band starts.

A chugging, slow, heavy guitar riff fills the Denny's, and the vocalist starts pacing back and forth saying, "what's up Denny's, what the fucks up Denny's?"

Great.

Her "date" is in the middle of the dining room going to war with an invisible army, every now and again he runs to the people standing off to the side and sucker punches them.

A guy in camo and a shirt that says Shattered Realm is just walking around rubbing his knuckles and punching people in the face.

The first song ends, Dana knows she's going to slip out after she eats. This stranger's feelings aren't that important to her.

The singer paces back and forth again, this time he says, "this song is about brotherhood."

The people in the pit go absolutely batshit and start punching, kicking, spinning, and shoving people on the outside.

How the hell does this place stay in business? She thinks as she makes eye contact with a nice-looking older couple in the back just trying to enjoy their meals.

It's still a Denny's.

When she turns back around a huge guy in a tank top is holding her food that the waiter must have just dropped off.

He yells, "meat is murder!" and then slams the plate on the ground.

That's the final fucking straw.

You can insult me, you can make old people uncomfortable, you can act a fool in Denny's, but do NOT fuck with someone's Eggs Over My Hammy.

Dana stands up, pulls her leg back, and sends it shooting forward into the guy's groin. He closes his eyes and falls off to the side of the table.

She sees a waiter staring at her in shock. She looks at this poor soul just trying to get through a workday and says, "he's paying. And if he doesn't tip, kick him again."

She calls Allie when she's outside.

"That was AWFUL."

"Same here. I left twenty minutes ago when my date admitted to having an unhealthy obsession with *The King of Queens*."

"Ouch."

"Told me all about this show. Don't get me wrong, I think Leah Remini is stunning, and the show is ok… but goddamn."

"Want to meet up tomorrow night?"

"I have my last date."

"Ok, no worries."

"Do you want to go on it with me?"

Eleven:
Fuck off, Jerry.

Dana and Allie make eye contact from across the room.

Allie's last date is a guy wearing camo pants and a red shirt.

Holy shit it's THIS guy again. Dave or whatever his name is.

Dana yells, "ALLIE!" and runs over to her.

Allie is already standing ready to embrace the hug.

Dave just shakes his head; he knows his date is over.

"You want to take my seat?" he asks. "We ordered a large pepperoni to split."

"Nah," says Dana, "I think I'll just sit with you both!"

Dave grumbles under his breath.

"So, how's the date going you two?"

"Dave was just telling me all about

abortion!" says Allie.

"Oh he does NOT like that does he?"

"Not at all. Calls people baby killers and stuff."

"Dave!"

Dave just sits there rubbing his temples.

"What do you have going on in the pants department?" Dana asks.

"It's tactical camo."

"Are you looking to hide your legs in the pizza place?"

"I didn't even know he HAD legs!" says Allie. "That's some damn good camo!"

"A red shirt and camo? Come on, Dave."

"Please…" says Dave rubbing his head. Dana gets the vibe he's praying to naked Donald Trump swaddled in a confederate flag to make her go away.

"Splitting the pizza, huh?" Dana says. "Must be going pretty good then?"

"It was until you came barreling in here on your liberal horse so you can look down on us."

"You've been doing most of the talking

then?"

"He has," says Allie.

"I can't take this," Dave says standing up to leave.

"What would you have me do, Dave?" Dana says. "Not eat? I can't help that- oh nevermind, he's left."

Allie and Dana hold back their laughter as a humiliated man wearing cargo pants leaves the pizza place frustrated.

They split the pizza, but also order some cheese sticks. Dana says that you can't have a meal at a place with cheese sticks and not order cheese sticks.

They talk and laugh through their meal about the awful experience this whole Ten-in-Ten thing has been.

Dana watches as Allie bites into a cheese stick, the cheese stringing out as she pulls it away. She watches as her eyes grow bigger and bigger the further the cheese stretches.

She's absolutely gone from a little crush, to thinking she's in love with this woman.

One date, one night, and some mutual

dating trauma really did bring them together.

They're holding hands across the table and talking about having a movie night when a man walks up and says, "Yo! Allie! Whoop Whoop! Where you been?"

Allie cringes and tries to hide it but says, "Hey, Jerry, I've been around. Just sort of doing my own thing, you know?"

"Yeah, yeah, the crew missed you last week. The show was dope. I'm still trying to get the Faygo outta my hair."

"Yuck. Sorry I missed it."

"How's your pops? Mans was at the shop like, a month ago? Picked up a few He-Man figs and bounced. I told him we all missed you at the Gathering too."

"Yeah, yeah, he told me. So, uh, Jerry, I'm kind of on a date right now, but I'll stop by, ok?"

"Hell yeah, girl! Whoop whoop!"

"Yeah… whoop whoop."

Allie looks down at the table as if the most embarrassing thing to ever happen to her has just happened. Jerry came in like a dad picking up his teenage daughter listening to Danzig. He was the mom blowing her seventeen years old son a kiss in front of his crush.

"He was…" starts Dana, "interesting."

"He owns the toy shop up town."

"The Klown Kar? What's with the K's? One more and he'd be in SERIOUS trouble."

"He's into the whole, you know, juggalo thing."

"Oh, right."

The tension is so thick in this moment you'd need a jackhammer to break through. Dana resists every urge of her being to ask if Allie is in fact also into the whole, you know, Juggalo thing. Instead, she smiles, eats more food and talks about how Barb collects wrestling figures.

"Barb, your roommate?" asks Allie.

"The one and only."

"She also sounds… interesting."

"Ugh, you have NO idea. She's a bit of a

chore. But she's my closest friend. You didn't see her last time because she's been seeing this guy that works at Starbucks pretty steady. She gives him free coffee, has a house, and apparently, he's good at the extracurricular stuff judging by how many nights she stays with him."

"I was starting to wonder if I should worry about Barb."

"Allie… is that a hint of jealousy I detect?"

"Of course, it is, Barb sounds great. How could I not feel threatened by a woman with a bitchin' wrestling figure collection."

"Want to come over and see if she's there?"

"Sure."

Interlude for another awkward sex scene.

Barb was there.

She said hi and hugged Allie.

Then she threatened to end her life if she hurt Dana.

Then her boyfriend emerged naked from her bedroom.

She announced they would be going to his place.

She slapped Dana on the butt, threw her a wink and a thumbs up, then headed out the door with her little barista in tow.

Dana forced Allie to watch the *Critters* franchise all the way through while they got better and better at this whole sex thing.

The bra wasn't an issue this time.

Neither was the shirt.

They had just started to get the hang of it when Dana noticed Allie had a tattoo on her left thigh…

A tattoo of a spiky haired guy carrying a hatchet…

Twelve:
Dad bod

"Do you wanna come with me and meet my dad?

Ten words that were spoken earlier today that sent Dana into an emotional spiral.

Should I be meeting him this early?

Does this mean Allie LOVES me and not just LIKES me?

Do I LOVE Allie and not just LIKE her?

What the Hell should I wear?

Is he going to meet me at the door with a gun and ask what my intentions are with his daughter?

Does this mean she needs to meet my parents?

"Yeah, totally!" she had said. "I'm, like, so prepared for that and believe fully that our relationship has reached that point."

"Ok…" Allie said. "You're overthinking

it. Maybe not. I think I may be in love with you, and planning to marry you, so I feel like this isn't a big deal."

"No, no. It's not. I think I'm in love with you."

"Did we just have a Hallmark Christmas movie moment?"

"I think we totally did."

As they pull up to Allie's dad's place, Allie says, "ok, now listen. He has a lot, I mean A LOT, of He-Man stuff in here. Do not judge."

When they go in Dana has to admit this is the most He-manliest of all He-Man places she's ever seen.

The TV is enclosed in Castle freaking Greyskull.

Allie's dad looks like a dad.

How else do you describe a sixty-year-old man wearing a plaid shirt, jeans, and those bad ass white New Balance that are made for mowing a lawn or grilling?

He hugs Allie and looks Dana up and down.

"So," he says, sending Dana's mind into repeating *dontsayitdontsayitdontsayit.* "What are your intentions with my daughter?"

Goddamnit.

"Sir," Dana says. "I intend to buy her Castle Greyskull."

He rubs Allie's shoulder and says proudly, "you've finally brought one home I like."

They share a moment of laughter and catching up on TV shows they watch together but in different places. Dana just sits and takes it all in with a smile.

She starts looking around the room and noticing pictures of Allie from when she was younger.

In a couple she has a shirt with the same logo she has tattooed on her thigh.

In a few she has weird braids that are trying to be dreadlocks.

In one she's kissing a bottle of Faygo.

In another…

Sweet Jesus she's painted like a clown.

That crazy goth woman was right, thinks Dana, *life IS pointless, and the love of my life is a Juggalo.*

She makes it through the hour visit all smiles and positivity. Allie's dad picks on her from time to time by calling her a clown.

Dana cringes every time.

What could be worse than this?

No wonder that guy kept saying whoop whoop.

Allie is a full on Faygo drinking, hatchet wielding, pretending to be a serial killer, bad music listening, walking on Washington to prove they aren't a gang- JUGGALO.

Dana feels like she's just found out Allie is married and has five kids. The world is spinning. What the Hell is she going to do? She can't go to these concerts and hang out with these people.

When she was in high school there was this girl who was fifteen and dating a twenty-two-year-old. He had a hatchback that was always filled with cigarette smoke. When they would roll up to school to drop her off it would pour out like something inside was on fire.

The music that came from the little car sounded like someone rapping over carnival tunes.

A month after the drop offs started happening, the girl was sent to a different school and the guy was arrested.

Hopefully for the age difference and not just being a Juggalo, although both should be punishable; just on a different scale.

Allie asks if Dana wants to see what her dad has done to her room.

Dana agrees, even though she's shit scared she's going to find a million cigarette butts inside of empty bottles of Faygo.

The room is just filled with *Star Wars* toys.

Thank God.

Allie's dad tells Dana all about the section dedicated to Rose Tico and how wrong the franchise treated her character in *The Rise of Skywalker.*

Dana agrees.

She really does.

Rose was by far the best *Star Wars* character because she represented the fans. Imagine, a *Star Wars* fan getting recruited to the rebellion. That was Rose. It was beautiful and perfect and poignant and so on brand.

That's what she says to Matt, Allie's dad.

After visiting for another hour, they leave.

Dana doesn't know how to address the clown painted elephant in Allie's car, so she doesn't.

Allie, however, can tell something is wrong, so she says, "Dana, I can't help but notice something went weird here. What was it? Too soon?"

"No, perfect timing honestly. Completely perfect timing. Your dad is amazing."

"He thinks he is."

"He is."

"I think so."

"You should."

"Good."

"Great."

"Awesome."

"Are you a Juggalo?"

Allie closes her eyes and exhales hard out of her nose.

"You know," she says. "I was wondering when that would come up."

"Well?"

"Would that be the worst thing in the world?"

"It wouldn't be the best."

"Well, you're in luck. I am a recovering Juggalo."

"Meaning?"

"Meaning I used to be. About two years ago. Before Covid."

"Covid killed your inner Juggalo?"

"No, self-reflection did that."

"Go on."

"I realized I was being rebellious. My

dad didn't care what movies I liked, he didn't care that I was gay, he was OVERLY supportive of all of this."

"Shouldn't he be?"

"Oh, yeah. I love him for it now. But at thirteen? You want to piss your parents off."

"So you became a Juggalo."

"Actually, the term for women is Juggalette."

Dana just stares.

"Ok," says Allie. "Is that some sort of deal breaker? I thought we had something hella good going here. I took you to meet my dad, I assumed I was going to meet your parents soon. I thought this was going great."

"It is… I just… I don't know."

"Somehow every great moment we've had doesn't matter because I used to like the Insane Clown Posse?"

"See… that's just… like… a lot."

"Ok. I thought this whole being overly judgey of your dates was a gimmick you had going. I thought we were both just playing around. I'm not sure now."

"Are you saying I'm judgmental?"

"You are being, REALLY, judgey about a dumb style of music I used to like."

"Why aren't you into it now?"

"Over Covid, I didn't go to the Gathering, their big music festival, and I realized I was just keeping up appearances to keep my friends around. They weren't even really that close of friends; we just drove to the Gathering together and went to shows. All they ever wanted to do was be drunk or high. I'm cool with both in moderation, but it was a lot more enjoyable to focus on the things I really enjoy, like movies and music I actually enjoy. I haven't listened to any of that stuff since I was sixteen."

"Are they still your friends?"

"Not really, we grew apart and now I don't really have friends. Why are we talking about this like it was a drug addiction?"

"You were a Juggalo, Allie."

"Ok. And?"

"I don't know."

"And you're pretty full of judgement for a woman who is in love with her roommate."

"Holy shit. Do you really think that? That's… no."

"I don't believe it. I just wanted you to see what this all feels like."

"I think this conversation is over."

And it was over.

It was over for three days.

Thirteen:
Cotton Candy Flavored Soda

Barb came barging into Dana's room yelling, "ALRIGHT, BITCH. GET UP. WE'RE GOING OUT."

Dana couldn't be bothered to even roll over. She has been laying in the same spot in bed for three days straight. She refuses to move. Kurt the Third has toughed it out with her but every now and again needed out to use the restroom.

She'd let him out, here the scratch scratch of the litter box and then his little feet coming back to nurse his momma back to emotional stability.

Barb grabs the blanket Dana is on and pulls it toward her causing Dana to roll onto the floor.

"Listen," Barb says, "you judgmental turd. This is your fault. What does it matter if Allie was into something you think is embarrassing. My boyfriend is into CrossFit, do you know how embarrassing THAT is."

"He's your boyfriend now?"

"Hell yeah he is. I'm not letting that free coffee and prime time you know what get away anytime soon."

Dana starts crying again, through her tears and mumbling she says, "I wish Allie was still my girlfriend."

"Jesus Christ, have you tried calling her?"

"No."

"Why not?"

"Because I drank Faygo."

"And?"

"It was actually pretty good."

She barely chokes out the last line through her sobbing.

Barb shakes her head and leaves the room saying, "ten minutes, then we'll go to whatever place you want for dinner, I'll buy."

Dana lays there covering her face in a lake of tears that could really just be prevented by her saying sorry.

She won't do it though, it's like some sort of emotional blockage has happened and she can't do it.

She's being held back by juggalophobia.

It's a very specific phobia, she's as afraid of clown painted people as most people are of spiders.

She thinks there's a Pennywise joke in there somewhere but can't make the time to find it.

She's not afraid of the juggalos, it's more she's worried her girlfriend may be fascinated by magnets and not really know how they work.

She decides if she's going to wallow in her pain and Barb wants to go out; she'll take Barb somewhere so painful and emotionally draining that Barb will understand the bleak emptiness living inside her thanks to an ex-Juggalo named Allie, and a pretty damn decent tasting

Cotton Candy soda by Faygo.

They'll go to the goth club.

She throws on her finest Fields of the Nephilim shirt and heads into the living room.

"Oh, goddamnit," says Barb, "not the Fields of the Nephilim shirt. You really are going through it."

"If I were going through anymore it, Stephen King would have written it."

"He did."

"I know, that's the point of the play on words, Barb."

"Dana, I love you, but you fucking suck. You should only be so lucky that Allie even looked your way."

"Barb, you're a shallow asswipe."

"And we're back."

They take Barb's car to the club, when they park Barb takes a deep breath and applies some black lipstick to try to fit in.

"Hey, Barb," says Dana. "Do you know how magnets work?"

Fourteen:

Always trust a Roland…

Unless it's the first time you

meet him, and your name is

Jake.

"Does this place play anything other than Bauhaus?" Dana yells at the bartender.

He shrugs back and passes her the two beers she ordered.

Satan's Blackened Stout.

Supposedly the darkest beer on the market.

Considering it looked like someone poured black hair dye into mud, Dana had to assume that was the truth.

She sits both down at the small booth her and Barb are sitting in.

Barb isn't there because she's busy

dancing the same Bauhaus song this place plays on repeat.

Maybe it ISN'T the exact same song, but a bunch of songs that sound similar? With the bass up this high-

She's distracted from that thought by Barb using her teeth to take a glow stick from another woman's mouth.

Jesus Christ, Barb. Can't you keep it in your pants for one evening?

She sips the toxic sludge masked as beer and thinks about how maybe that gloomy girl had everything right.

Not only was Allie a Juggalo, but life IS a big dark lonely abyss.

She's busy wallowing in her own self-pity when none other than Roland flops down across from her.

"Your girl is stealing my girl!" he yells.

"I don't have a girl," Dana replies. "My life is one big dark lonely abyss."

"That's dramatic! Who's the girl with Jenna that you came in with?"

Dana takes in the situation, sure enough,

Barb is dancing with Jenna.

Jenna is smiling.

Weird.

She shrugs at Roland and takes a sip of mud in a glass.

Jenna and Barb fall into the booth beside Roland. Jenna looks at Dana and says, "wow! You look depressed. Wanna talk about it?"

Dana flips her off.

"You know each other?" Barb asks.

"Yeah," says Jenna. "Dana was a horrible date. But if it wasn't for her, Roland and I wouldn't be together."

Dana shakes her head back and forth; she wants the three smiling dipshits to know she's pissed.

"What happened with Allie?" asks Jenna.

"You should know," replies Dana.

"The Juggalo thing?"

"You were right. She was a Juggalo."

"Psssshhhhh! Roland is a gamer nerd who started coming here to get a big titty goth GF."

"Yeah, I know. Looks like it worked."

Roland looks at Jenna's chest and shakes his head yes like an overexcited teenage boy.

"She never would have given me the chance," Roland says. "But she didn't want to be a judgmental asshole like you!"

Dana looks at Jenna.

Jenna shrugs as if to say, "yah, so what?"

"The point is," Roland says. "Maybe don't be so judgmental."

"You really were kind of a bitch," says Jenna.

Barb says, "she can totally be like that sometimes."

"Message your Juggalo," Jenna says nodding at the phone in front of Dana. "Meet up with her tonight. If I can sort of like Roland, you can be ok with a Juggalo."

"Actually," says Dana smiling. "The term for women is Juggalette. And she's recovering. You're still lame."

Dana smiles and nods at Jenna in a silent thank you.

She texts Allie.

Fifteen:
Loaf of meat in the rain.

Dana stands outside the diner where she first met Allie.

She's holding flowers, a six pack of beer, and a Blu-ray of *The Alien Dead*.

A car pulls up, Allie gets out of it and tips the Uber driver in cash.

She pauses and stares at Dana.

They smile and hug as rain pours down around them.

"MMFCL," says Dana.

Allie laughs and shakes her head while saying, "MMFCL."

As they kiss a man rides a bicycle behind them.

He pauses and shakes up a can of soda before opening it.

As the soda pours down on Dana and Allie with the rain, he sings *I Would do Anything for Love* by Meatloaf.

Thank you stuff after the book...

Breanna, thank you for putting up with all
the times I say glizzy in a day.
Mercedes Varnado/Mone, thank you for
being my hero and inspiring me daily.

Thank you to the following cool AF
people
Just write your name here so I donut
accidentally forget anyone plz. K thx.

———————————————

About Damien Casey

One time, Danzig went to a wrestling
show. There's photographic proof of it.
Damien Casey writes books.

<u>ALSO BY DAMIEN CASEY</u>

<u>Coffin Dodger</u>

When your favorite actors aren't acting, they're dealing with ghost-snakes, giant crocodiles, spiders with human faces, and cults kidnapping them. One of these cults kidnaps a group of actors from a cult classic horror series. This cult forces the group to play a game where they have to face their biggest fears in order to gain eternal life. They don't even want eternal life. It's all pretty inconvenient.

28 Days Sassier

It's a post-apocalyptic Bigfoot book.

Not an interlude for an awkward sex scene

Allie and Dana had a lot more arguments.

Some were about how Allie used to be a juggalette.

Some were about how judgy Dana was.

They got married anyway.

Neither their son or daughter became Juggalos; they are sort of judgy though.

Barb married her barista.

They have four kids.

Jenna and Roland got married.

Their son makes fun of their wedding pictures in which they're wearing all black and holding glowsticks.

www.ingramcontent.com/pod-product-compliance
Lightning Source LLC
Chambersburg PA
CBHW071347150726
47997CB00002B/886